DIAL BOOKS FOR YOUNG READERS
Published by the Penguin Group
Penguin Group (USA) LLC
375 Hudson Street
New York, New York 10014

USA / Canada / UK / Ireland / Australia / New Zealand / India / South Africa / China

penguin.com

A Penguin Random House Company

Library of Congress Cataloging-in-Publication Data

Schaapman, Karina, 1960- author, illustrator
[Muizenhuis. English]
The Mouse Mansion / by Karina Schaapman.   pages cm
Originally published in the Netherlands in 2011.
Summary: Best friends Sam and Julia love spending their days exploring the many rooms
and secret hiding places of the Mouse Mansion, where they live with their families.
ISBN 978-0-8037-4049-5 (hardcover : alk. paper) [1. Best friends—Fiction.
2. Friendship—Fiction. 3. Dwellings—Fiction. 4. Mice—Fiction.] I. Title.
PZ7.S32787Mou 2014   [Fic]--dc23   2013044458

Manufactured in China on acid-free paper
1 3 5 7 9 10 8 6 4 2

Designed by Mina Chung
Text set in Walbaum MT STD

The MOUSE MANSION

Karina Schaapman

Dial Books for Young Readers

An imprint of Penguin Group (USA) LLC

Table of Contents

Sam and Julia

Here are Sam and Julia. Shall we say hello?

Hello, Sam. Hello, Julia. Sam and Julia live in the Mouse Mansion, and they are best friends.

Julia lives on the top floor in a little apartment with her mom. Her mom says that Julia is too curious for such a little mouse, but Julia just says that she likes big adventures.

And Sam, Julia's best friend, lives right in the very middle of the Mouse Mansion. He has a big family. He has a mom, a dad, lots of brothers and sisters, two grandpas and two grandmas, two aunts, and an uncle. Sam is a little bit shy, but Julia looks after him. They have lots of fun together.

Most of all, Sam and Julia like exploring. Let's see what adventures they find in the Mouse Mansion.

The Secret Hiding Place

The Mouse Mansion is busy with mice running here, there, and everywhere, but there's one special place that only Sam and Julia know about. It's their favoritest place in the whole world. Look, there it is, just under the stairs. Sam and Julia call it the secret hidey-place. It's a very good place for thinking up magical make-believe adventures.

It's small and cozy and just the right size for the two friends. It's a bit gloomy, but don't worry, it's not dark all the time. Every time someone runs up the stairs a little light flashes on and then, ten seconds later, off it goes again.

But the best thing about the secret hidey-place is that it is very good for hiding things. One day, Julia found a wooden box, and then Sam found a loose plank in the floor. Underneath the plank was a hole just big enough for the box. Well, what a perfect place for treasures!

Now Sam and Julia keep all their secret things in the box—bits of string, old coins, favorite buttons, and lots of other special treasures. And because the box has a lock, it is the most secret place of all.

The Ragman

The Mouse Mansion always has lots of interesting visitors, but Julia's favorite is definitely the ragman. Once a week, he trudges past the Mouse Mansion with his cart and collects all sorts of things from the recycling room—old clothes, bits of paper, tufts of wool, and even old scraps of metal.

Here he is. "Rags, rags, bring out your rags!" Listen, can you hear him, too?
    Sam and Julia are very excited and quickly rush to the door of the recycling room. *Knock, knock, knock.* "Can we come and help?"
    But it's awfully quiet.
    So Julia knocks again. Very loudly. *BANG, BANG, BANG!* And whoops, she bangs so hard that the door bursts open all by itself!
    "Never mind," says Sam. And he calls out "Hello, is anyone here?"
    Julia scurries up a super-high pile of papers to get a better view. And there he is, there's the ragman!
    "Hello! Can we help?" says Julia.
    "Yes, of course, you can," the ragman says. "Julia, why don't you collect the clothes, and Sammy, you gather up the papers. I'll carry the metal myself."
    An hour later everything is neat and tidy. Sam and Julia are very pleased with their hard work. The job is finished, and the ragman gives them twenty-five cents to share. "See you next time!" he says.
    Twenty-five cents! Sam and Julia can't believe their luck and quickly rush away to put the money in their secret treasure box.

Pancakes

But what's that? Hmm. There's a delicious smell in the Mouse Mansion, and Sam and Julia know exactly what it is. Sam's grandma is making pancakes!

They both rush up to the apartment as fast as they can. Sam's grandma tosses a pancake up in the air, and it flips up and over and then lands back in the pan. Perfect!

"They look delicious," says Julia.

But just then the phone rings. "I won't be a minute," Grandma says as she hurries away. "Can you watch the pan?"

Sam and Julia start to laugh and chat, and then they remember to look at the pan. Suddenly there's smoke everywhere!

17

"Uh-oh," says Sam.

"Don't worry," says Julia, "this is easy peasy." And she picks up the pan and tosses the pancake up in the air, just like Grandma.

But, oh dear, look out, Sam! Julia tosses the pancake too hard, and it lands right on Sam's head. *SPLAT!*

"Ouch! It's hot!" he cries.

Julia grabs the pancake and, with a flick of her wrist, plunks it back in the pan, just as Grandma comes back into the room.

"How clever you are," she says. "You flipped the pancake all by yourself! From now on you can help me make *all* the pancakes."

At last, the pancakes are ready, and it's time to eat.

"I'm starving," says Julia. "Can I have one with powdered sugar, please?"

Julia shakes and shakes the box of sugar and suddenly there's powdered sugar everywhere. Whoops! Then Sam starts to sneeze and that makes things worse. Oh dear! What a pair of messy mice.

"I wish every day could be a pancake day," says Sam.

"So I do!" says Julia.

And with their tummies full and their hearts glad, soon it's time for bed.

The Musician

The Mouse Mansion is full of noises and sounds, but when Julia wakes up today there's a new noise, something Julia has never heard before. It's a horrible noise. All squeaky and sharp and low and grumbly, too.

"What *is* that?" says Julia, and she sticks her paws in her ears.

And to make things worse, she can't find Sam either. "Sam, Sammy!" she yells. "Where are you?"

Julia races up and down the staircases, but she can't find Sam anywhere. Just then, she spots a violinist in the music room. So that's where the strange sound is coming from!

But it's a truly awful noise, and it gives Julia the shivers. "Ugh. I really don't like that," she says, and runs as far away as she can.

Surprise!

Suddenly Julia stops to think. Maybe Sam is at home? So she rushes straight there and, of course, there he is.

"I've been looking for you everywhere!" says Julia. "Can you come and play?"

"No, I can't," says Sam excitedly, "because look who arrived last night—two new baby brothers *and* a baby sister!"

"Oh, triplets!" cries Julia. "Aren't they cute?"

The new babies are tiny and very, very sweet.

"I would love a little brother or sister," says Julia.

"Well," says Sam, "they are cute, but they cry *all* the time and they poop a *lot*."

"Right, Sam, you can help change their diapers!" says his mom.

Sam looks so miserable that Julia bursts out laughing!

In the end, they all help change the diapers, and then Sam and Julia go out to play.

Little Sophie's Birthday

Just as Sam and Julia are heading out to play, they remember something very important. It's Sophie's birthday! Sophie is Sam's cousin, and she is having her very first birthday party today.

They dash up the stairs and arrive at Sophie's house just in time for cake. Phew, isn't that lucky!

Everyone sings while Sophie sits in her high chair and shouts, "Cake, cake, cake!" which makes Sam and Julia laugh.

"First we'll put your bib on," says Sam's auntie, "and then you can blow out the candle."

But Sophie is *very* little and even though she blows very hard—*Pfffffffff!*—she can't quite manage it.

"I'll help!" says Julia. And with one big blow, the candle is out. The little mice sit at the table and soon dig into big slices of delicious birthday cake.

"Mmm, strawberry," says Sam. "My favorite."

"Look, Sophie," says Sam. "I brought you a present."

Little Sophie unwraps it and inside is a beautiful spinning top. Sam and Julie show Sophie how it works, and together they play with Sophie's new toys. She has a new set of building blocks and a hammer and Peg Board, too.

What a lucky little mouse!

Soon little Sophie has had enough of playing and starts to yawn.

"It must be time for her afternoon nap," says Auntie. "Come on, little one, time to sleep."

Julia and Auntie take Sophie upstairs to the bedroom, but Sophie does *not* want to go to bed. Auntie sings a lullaby, but Sophie just shouts, "Book, book, book!" So Julia reads her a story while Auntie rocks the crib, and soon little Sophie is fast asleep.

"Will you come and play with Sophie again?" says Auntie.

Julia replies very quickly, "Yes, please!" She loves feeling part of a big family.

"And can we play here in the bedroom?" says Julia. "On the big bed?"

"Of course you can," says Auntie. "Sophie would love that." And then Sam shouts up the stairs. "Julia!
Are you coming? Let's go and play."

"Coming!" calls Julia. "Bye-bye, Auntie. Oh, can I call you Auntie, too?"

"Of course!"

Sam and Julia go and play outside until dusk falls on Mouse Mansion, and finally it is time to go to their
little mouse beds.

Hoisting Time

The next day is a very unusual day. It is hoisting time, and that means the children are not allowed to play on the stairs for a whole week. Sam and Julia know all about hoisting because Sam's dad explained exactly what happens.

At the top of the house is a great big loft. This is where the mice of the Mouse Mansion store all their food, and during the first week of spring and the last week of autumn, large boxes of food and barrels of lemonade are carefully hoisted up to the loft to be stored. But be careful, it is very dangerous! At any moment, a barrel could slip from the rope hoist and tumble all the way down the stairs. Little mice are definitely not allowed.

Julia would love to explore the loft. But she knows she is not allowed, and she also knows that Sam would never dare.

Sam and Julia agree that hoisting time is very dull indeed for little mice who just want to have big adventures.

Laundry

At long last! Hoisting time is over! But before
Sam and Julia can go and explore, there are
mouse errands to do. Sam always helps his
mom with the washing, and today Julia is
helping, too.

Sam fills the washing machine with clothes,
and it's Julia's job to put the washing detergent
in. Except that Julia doesn't really know how
much soap is needed. I'll just put in the whole
box, she thinks to herself, just to be on the
safe side.

Sam presses the ON button, and they watch
the clothes go round and round. All of a
sudden, the machine starts banging. Very
loudly.

"Uh-oh," says Julia. "What's happening?"

"I don't know." Sam says, and looks worried.
"It shouldn't be making that noise. I'll go and
ask my mom." And off he runs.

Oh no! Look at all that foam! Things are not
going very well *at all*.

"Help!" cries Julia. "Sam, Sammy!"

At last Sam comes back and presses the STOP button. And he's just in time, too. Julia is covered in suds from the tip of her tail to the top of her nose!

She starts laughing. "Look at me! I'm nice and clean, too."

"You're a very silly mouse," says Sam. "You put too much soap in the machine. Quick, how are we going to get rid of all this foam?"

"I've got an idea," says Julia. "Let's scoop it all into the bathtub and then we can wash it away."

It's a fine idea indeed. All the suds soon get washed away, and then Sam and Julia carefully dry the floor. Last of all, they hang out the wash and, just then, Sam's mom comes in.

"Oh, it smells lovely and fresh in here," she says. "And you've hung out all the clothes, too. What helpful little mice. Thank you!"

Uncle John Can Do Anything

Sam and Julia quickly head to the secret hidey-place, but something awful has happened. The special treasure box is broken. They can't open the lid!

"Oh dear, it must be the lock," says Julia. "Whatever are we going to do?" And she looks as if she might cry.

Sam hates seeing Julia upset, so he quickly says, "I know. Let's go and see Uncle John. He knows how to fix things. He's just the mouse we need."

They set off and soon find Uncle John in his storeroom.

"Hello," says Sam. "Can you help? Our special box is broken."

"Of course," says Uncle John. "Why don't you come through to my workshop and I'll see what I can do?"

Julia is hopping about from one foot to another. "But please don't peek inside," she says. "It's full of our secret treasure, and it's very special."

In the workshop, Uncle John pulls the broken key out of the lock with a pair of tongs. "Ah-ha!" he says. "Now we just need to find a new key." He pulls open a drawer and tries out a selection of keys one by one. Suddenly— *PING!*—the lock springs open. Uncle John has found the right key! The box works!

Julia is so excited she jumps up and down. "Thank you!" she cries. "Thank you."

The two little mice are *very* relieved. All their special treasures are safe again.

"We mustn't lose the key," says Julia. "We must find a hiding place for it."

"Yes, but where?" says Sam.

"What about your bedroom?" says Julia.

"My little brother might find it," says Sam. "What about *your* bedroom?"

"My mom is sure to find it," replies Julia. She thinks for a moment. "I know!" she exclaims, and she grabs Sam by the paw and rushes up to his bedroom.

In Sam's room, Julia climbs on his bed and places the key on top of a sloping roof beam. "Look," she says, "your little brother can't reach it there, and no one else can see it either. Now let's go and play!"

"Actually," says Sam, "do you mind if I finish reading my book first? I've just gotten to a really good part."

Julia doesn't mind at all, and she happily goes to play on her own.

Chicken Pox

The next day, Sam comes to knock on Julia's door and this time it's Julia who can't play. She has chicken pox. Poor Julia!

Chicken pox is very contagious and so she must stay in bed and is not allowed to play with anyone. Not even Sam. Julia doesn't want to play anyway.

Her head hurts with a fever and she has spots all over—on her tummy, legs, arms, and even her nose. And, oh dear, the spots are so itchy. Luckily Julia's mommy has just the thing. She picks some special mint leaves and crushes them into a paste to dab on the spots.

"There," she says, "that will make them feel better."

And of course, Julia's mommy is right.

Soon Julia does feel better, and she asks for a story. So Julia's mommy sits on the bed and tells the little mouse exciting stories full of princesses and kings and lands faraway.

With her head full of stories and moonlight and magic, Julia soon forgets that she feels bad, and after a little while falls fast asleep.

The Bakery

A week later, Julia is feeling much better and is busy playing with Sam in the Mouse Mansion, just as they always do. All of a sudden Julia remembers the twenty-five cents from the ragman.

"What shall we spend it on, Sam?" asks Julia.

"I know," says Sam. "Let's buy chocolate at the bakery."

Julia nods. "Yes, I'm hungry, too," she says

They quickly go and find the money, but because they don't want to spend it all at once, they leave fifteen cents at home.

Sam and Julia scamper down the stairs to the bakery. Mmmm, it smells so delicious. And look at all the lovely things on display. Yum!

Sam and Julia spend a long time deciding what they want until finally Julia says, "A bar of white chocolate with rice bubbles, please."

"Of course," says the baker. "That will be fifty cents please."

But oh dear, Sam and Julia only brought ten cents. It's not enough.

Julia counts her money again, just to make sure. "What shall we do, Sam?" she says.

"Is there anything we can buy for ten cents?" asks Sam.

"Well, I have some delicious broken cookies," says the baker.

"Perfect!" say Julia and Sam together.

"Mmmm. Look, Sam," says Julia. "There are pieces of ginger snaps *and* chunks of chocolate cookies, my favorite."

Sam's mouth is already watering. "Oh, and look," he says, "there's strawberry shortcake, too."

The two little mice wander along, happily munching and crunching on their treats until the sun sets and it's time for bed.

Grandpa the Sailor

The next morning dawns with a bright blue sky. It's another *very* good day for an adventure.

So Sam decides to take Julia to meet his grandpa. Sam's grandpa isn't an ordinary grandpa. Oh, no. Sam's grandpa is a sailor, full of exciting stories.

But Sam's grandpa lives on the top floor of the Mouse Mansion, at the very highest point. Can you see how steep the staircase is? Julia is very brave and doesn't mind the steps at all, but they are almost at the very top when Sam suddenly feels scared. It's so very high, and such a long way down.

"Don't worry, Sam," says Julia. "Just don't look down." And she holds her best friend's hand. In no time at all the two mice arrive.

When the weather is nice, Sam's grandpa sits outside mending fishing nets, or if it's stormy, he looks out at the ocean with his binoculars and watches the ships. But his favorite chair is empty today.

Julia knocks on the door anyway. "Sam's Grandpa, Sam's Grandpa!"

But there's no answer at all.

"Perhaps he's at the fish market," says Sam.

Poor Julia and poor Sam. Now they have to go all the way back down again!

Finally Sam and Julia arrive at the fish market, and there is Sam's grandpa!

"Look, Julia," says Sam. "There he is! The one with the sailing ship on his back!"

Sam's grandpa quickly turns around and waves at the little mice. Now Julia can see that he has a picture of an anchor on his arm *and* a pirate on his tummy!

Julia is very curious. "Why do you have all those drawings?" she asks. "What are they?"

Grandpa smiles. "They are not drawings," he says. "They're tattoos. And each one tells a story." Grandpa points to each tattoo, in turn, and tells Julia all about his travels: the time when he saw a gray-blue humpback whale and how he chased a band of evil pirates.

Julia's eyes grow big and round. "Golly," she says, "is that all true?"

"Of course it is," says Sam's grandpa, and he gives her a big wink.

The Shop That Sells Everything

They have just said good-bye to Sam's grandpa when Julia hears her mom calling.

"Julia, Julia, where are you?"

"Coming!"

Julia waves to Sam and dashes back home where she finds her mom holding fifty cents. "Can you pop to the shop and buy some soap for me?"

"Of course, Mama," says Julia, and she quickly skips away. Julia likes being helpful and loves going to the shop. It's the kind of shop that sells *everything*. She runs down the stairs, around the corner, up even more stairs until finally she runs through the archway into the shop. It's a very pretty shop with a blue-and-white-striped awning and lots of jars full of different things.

Phew. Julia's a bit out of breath, but she can't wait to help her mama. "Can I buy a piece of soap?" she asks the shopkeeper.

"What kind of soap do you want?" the shopkeeper asks. "Soap for the laundry, or for taking a bath, or soap that just smells lovely?"

But, oh dear, Julia can't remember what kind of soap her mom asked for. Luckily the shopkeeper is a very kind and friendly fellow. He gets out lots of different kinds of soap—rose, lavender, pine—and finally brings out a big block of white soap.

"Yes, that's it, that's the one!" Julia cries. "It's perfect for the laundry."

"That will be forty-five cents please," says the shopkeeper.

So Julia hands over fifty cents, and when the shopkeeper hands over the change, he gives her a licorice candy, too.

"Oh, thank you," says Julia, and off she dashes again.

Friday Night Dinner

It's nearly evening and Sam and Julia are visiting Sam's other auntie.

Every Friday evening Sam's auntie sets the table with her finest dishes and cutlery. Julia has never seen anything like it. There are beautiful dishes and plates, crystal glasses, and sparkling chandeliers, and oh, it all smells so delicious. The air is full of the scents of freshly baked bread and chicken soup.

Julia's tummy grumbles, and she reaches for a piece of bread.

"No, not yet," Sam says. "We mustn't eat until everyone is sitting down at the table and the candles have been lit."

Auntie comes in with an embroidered cloth that she lays over the bread.
And she explains to Julia exactly what happens on the Sabbath. "When the sun
goes down I will light the candles and we will sing a song. Then we will eat."

Julia knows it is a very special evening and is so glad to be invited.
The food looks delicious, but what she loves more is being all together
with Sam's family.

In fact, Sam is just like a big brother, and Julia gives her best friend a big smile.

A Rat on the Staircase

Later that night, everything is very quiet in the Mouse Mansion. The day is over, the mice are on their way to bed, and all is dark and quiet on the staircase.

For Julia and Sam, it's time for bed, too. But maybe, just maybe, there is time for one last game. They quickly hurry to the secret hidey-place when suddenly, Julia stops.

"*Sssssh*, look!" Julia whispers in a very quiet voice. Sam squeezes her arm. He has seen it, too. There is a very big, very black mouse sitting at the top of the stairs. Gulp.

"Is it a rat?" asks Julia.

"I think it might be," says Sam in a small quiet voice.

The mice are *very* scared. What are they going to do?

Slowly, slowly, Julia takes a step to the left. And the rat steps to the left, too. Then Julia slowly steps to the right and the rat does *exactly* the same thing. *Oh, no*, he won't let them pass!

"Help!" squeaks Julia.

Sam is so frightened he drops his lantern—*BANG!*—and the rat disappears completely! "Let's get out of here!" he cries, and quickly picks up his lantern. Suddenly the rat is back at the top of the stairs, even bigger and more enormous than before.

All of a sudden, Julia bursts out laughing. She knows what it is! "That's not a rat, Sam, it's my shadow! Look, I'll show you."

And Julia takes the lantern and stands behind Sam. Now it's Sam's shadow that appears on the stairs.

"Phew!" they both say, but Sam still doesn't feel like laughing—he has never been so frightened in his life. He *hates* rats.

Bedtime

It's very late now. The two mice have a special lantern which glows brightly to light the way home and soon Sam hears his mom calling him. "Sam, Sam! Come home. It's time for bed!"

Neither mouse wants to go home—it's been such a fun day—but they both know that tomorrow will be full of adventures, too.

"Night, night, Julia," says Sam.

"Good night," says Julia. "Shall we play again tomorrow?"

"Of course!" cries Sam as he scampers home. "We shall go exploring!"

Julia then skips home herself and starts to tells her mother all about her day.

All around her the Mouse Mansion and all the little mice who live there go very quietly and very gently to sleep.